Windy Miller and the Great Race

A CAMBERWICK GREEN STORY

By Richard Mead
Based on a Channel Four Series

sapling

First Published in 1996 by Sapling, an imprint of
Boxtree Ltd, Broadwall House, 21 Broadwall,
London SE1 9PL

Copyright © Gordon Murray
(Trumptonshire) Ltd 1996

10 9 8 7 6 5 4 3 2 1

Designed and illustrated by
Simon Girling & Associates
Printed and bound in Great Britain by
Cambus Litho Ltd, East Kilbride.

ISBN: 0 7522 0362 2

A CIP catalogue entry for
this book is available from
the British Library

Farmer Bell was very happy. His brand new truck had arrived today and he was driving it around Camberwick Green. He beeped his horn, so everyone would stop and look at him. "I'll go to the garage and show my lovely truck to Mr Crockett," thought Farmer Bell. "I need to buy some petrol too."

3

Farmer Bell arrived at the same time as Dr Mopp. Mr Crockett, the garage owner, came out to serve them.

"The best petrol for my best customers," he smiled, filling Dr Mopp's tank first. "There we are, sir!"

"Thank you," shouted Farmer Bell and sped away. But he hadn't been given any petrol!

"Oh dear," said Mr Crockett. "His tank is nearly empty!"

FB 1

5

Farmer Bell whizzed along the country lanes until he met Windy Miller. Windy was going to the shops on his tricycle.

"Could you bring me a sack of corn this afternoon, please?" asked Windy. "Of course," replied Farmer Bell. "But if you had a truck instead of a tricycle, you could fetch it yourself!"

"Oh no!" laughed Windy. "My tricycle is much better than your truck. It never breaks down or makes horrid noises. I'm sure it could race against anything!"

"Then you can race me and my truck this afternoon!" suggested Farmer Bell. "If you win, I'll give you the sack of corn free."
Windy agreed and waved goodbye as he pedalled away.

Farmer Bell returned to Camberwick Green and bought a stamp at the Post Office from Mrs Dingle. She was very excited to hear his news.

Later Dr Mopp and Mrs Honeyman visited the Post Office. Mrs Dingle told them about the great race. It wasn't long before everyone in Camberwick Green was talking about it!

At two o'clock that afternoon the soldiers from Pippin Fort arrived at Colley's Mill to start the race. Captain Snort explained the rules to Windy and Farmer Bell.

"You can start when the cannon is fired," he said.
"The first person to reach Mickey Murphy's Bakery
is the winner!"

BOOM! Windy heard the cannon and began pedalling. The wheels on his tricycle spun round as he travelled down the lane.
Farmer Bell followed behind him.

"My car is much more powerful than his tricycle," he said to himself. "I can pass him whenever I want!"

Farmer Bell was so sure he would win, he even stopped to post a letter! Then he got back in his truck and set off at top speed. He drove past Pippin Fort. He drove past Mr Crockett's garage. And he drove past Windy puffing and panting on his tricycle.

Poor Windy - he was completely out of breath!
But he wasn't going to stop until he had reached
the finishing post.

A big crowd was waiting outside Mickey's Bakery. Dr Mopp was the first person to spot Farmer Bell's truck coming towards them. Everyone began clapping and shouting.

But then the cheering stopped. Farmer Bell's truck had stopped! He had parked it outside the Post Office and was walking inside. "Just time to buy some writing paper," he thought.

Two minutes later, Farmer Bell climbed into his truck.
"I'll stay here until Windy overtakes me," he decided. "Then I'll show him how fast my truck really is!"
He didn't have to wait very long.
"Look, here comes Windy," shouted Mickey Murphy. "And now he's in the lead!"

Farmer Bell watched the tricycle go past. Then he turned the key to start the engine again. The truck crawled forward for a few seconds... and then just stopped!

Farmer Bell turned the key again but nothing happened. He looked up and saw the tricycle cross the finishing line. Windy was the winner and everyone was cheering!
Mr. Crockett walked over to the truck.

"You've run out of petrol," he explained to Farmer Bell. "You left my garage too soon!"
Farmer Bell laughed at the silly mistake he had made and went to congratulate Windy.

23

"Well done Windy," said Farmer Bell. "And here is your sack of corn."
"Thank you," Windy replied. "I knew I could trust my tricycle. People can run out of petrol - but they never run out of legs!"